**To the memory of Mutti, my beloved grandmother** *–S.M.*

**To Anna, the ice cream queen** *–J.D.*

tiger tales

**an imprint of ME Media, LLC**
**202 Old Ridgefield Road, Wilton, CT 06897**
**Published in the United States 2011**
**Text copyright ©2011 Steve Metzger**
**Illustrations copyright ©2011 Julie Downing**
**CIP data is available**
**Hardcover ISBN-13: 978-1-58925-096-3**
**Hardcover ISBN-10: 1-58925-096-6**
**Paperback ISBN-13: 978-1-58925-427-5**
**Paperback ISBN-10: 1-58925-427-9**
**Printed in China**
**LPP 0610**
**1 3 5 7 9 10 8 6 4 2**
**For more insight and activities, visit us at www.tigertalesbooks.com**

# THE ICE CREAM KING

by Steve Metzger       Illustrated by Julie Downing

tiger tales

On a hot day in July, Teddy Jones saw something that stopped him in his tracks.

"Look, Mom!" he exclaimed. "It's a **brand-new ice cream shop!** Can we go in? Can we, *please?*"

"Sure," said Teddy's mom.

Inside, Teddy looked at all the flavors on the big board. "Can I have anything I want?" he asked. "Just for me?" "Yes," said Teddy's mom. "Anything you want— just for you."

FLAVORS
Moon Crater Crunch
Peanut Butter Party
Double Double Fudge Fudge
Raspberry Rocket
Cookie Dough Castle
Marshmallow Mountain

As Teddy tried to decide,
the server put a paper crown
on his head, and . . .

**WOW! That's awesome, Teddy thought.
My mom said, "ANYTHING!"
Upon my throne of ice cream cones . . .**
I am the Ice Cream King!

Ice cream treats are all I see—
and they're all for me!

Inside my ice cream castle,
I slide down chocolate halls.
I pick out rainbow sprinkles
from mint-chip ice cream walls.

I slip and slide down Whipped Cream Lane,
then climb up Ice Cream Mountain.

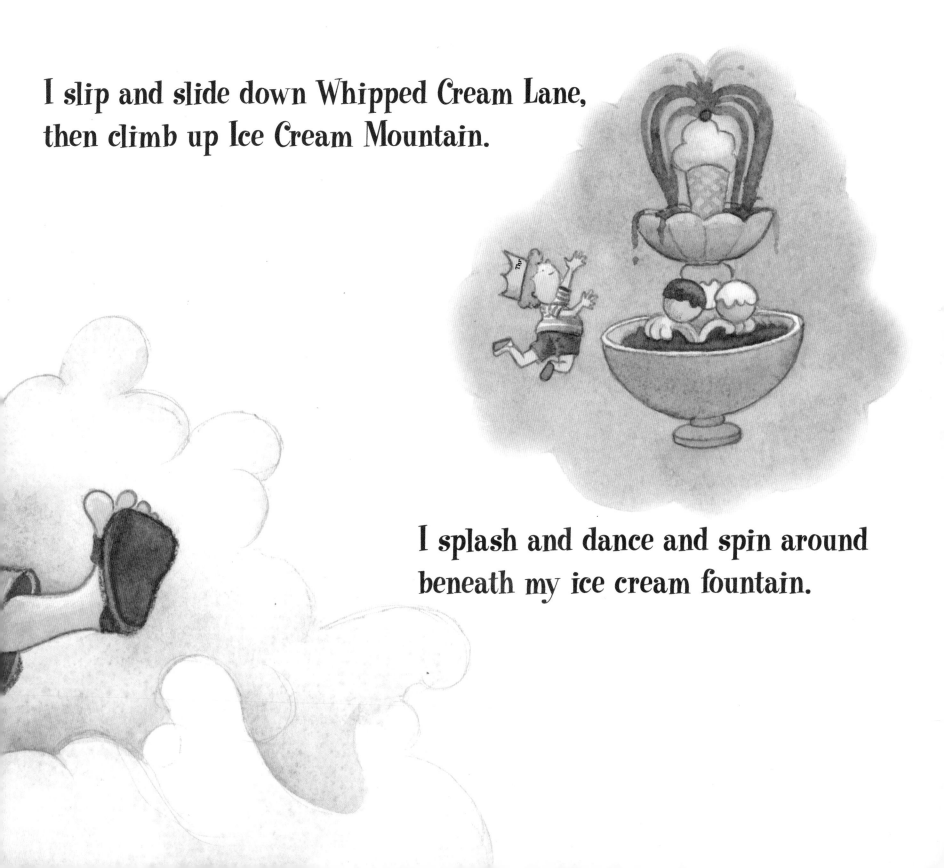

I splash and dance and spin around
beneath my ice cream fountain.

Aboard my silver sailboat,
I sail an ice cream sea.
I fish for nuts and cherries—
they're all for me, me, ME!

My very own volcano
shoots out vanilla fudge.
Today's the Ice Cream Festival,
and I'm the only judge.

I think there's something missing,
as I look around my throne,
and suddenly I notice that...

# I am all

# alone!

I dance and slide on ice cream.
I can even wear it.
But it would be much better
with somebody to share it.

**Teddy took off his crown. . . .**

"So, have you decided?" asked Teddy's mom.

"Yes," he said. "Please give me a banana split with strawberry and chocolate ice cream and lots and lots of hot fudge and whipped cream and sprinkles and . . . and . . . "

"And?" asked Teddy's mom.

"And?" asked the server.

"And . . . " Teddy said.

"Two spoons!"